MR. JELLY

by Roger Hargreaves

WORLD INTERNATIONAL
MANCHESTER

Poor Mr Jelly was frightened of everything and anything.

At the slightest little thing he would quiver and tremble and shake and turn to jelly.

So, it's not really surprising to find that Mr Jelly lives as far away from anybody that he can find.

In the middle of a wood, miles and miles from anywhere.

This story begins one morning when Mr Jelly was asleep.

It was a beautiful autumn morning. The sun was shining. The leaves on the trees had turned to a glorious red. And the wind stirred gently in the treetops.

A single leaf fell gently from the tree right outside Mr Jelly's house and quietly brushed against his bedroom window as it fell.

Mr Jelly awoke with a start.

"What's that terrible noise?" he cried. "Oh heavens! The house is falling down! Oh disaster! It's an earthquake! Oh calamity! It's the end of the world!"

And he hid under the bedclothes, trembling with fright.

After an hour, by which time he realised that his house wasn't falling down, and there wasn't an earthquake, and the world wasn't coming to an end, Mr Jelly peeped out from under the bedclothes.

"Phew," he said. "Thank goodness for that!"

And he got up and went downstairs to make his breakfast.

Mr Jelly poured some cornflakes out of a packet on to a plate.

Then he poured some milk on to the cornflakes.

Then he went to the cupboard to get some sugar.

Snap! Crackle! Pop! went the cornflakes in the milk.

"Oh goodness gracious!" cried Mr Jelly, diving under the kitchen table. "Oh dear! I hear guns! Oh calamity! It's war!"

But of course it wasn't.

And of course Mr Jelly eventually came out from under the table and ate up all his cornflakes.

After breakfast Mr Jelly thought that he'd go for a walk.

He was walking through the woods which surround his house when a worm poked his head out of the ground.

"Morning," said the worm cheerfully to Mr Jelly.

Mr Jelly nearly jumped out of his skin.

"What?" he shouted. "Who's there?" And then he saw the worm. "Oh good heavens! It's a snake! Oh dear! A man-eating snake! Oh calamity! I'm going to be eaten alive!" And he jumped up into a tree.

"What a performance," commented the worm, and went back into his hole.

After an hour Mr Jelly felt brave enough to climb down from the tree and continue his walk.

Eventually he came out of the other side of the wood and into a field.

Mr Jelly glanced nervously around.

It was an empty field.

Or was it?

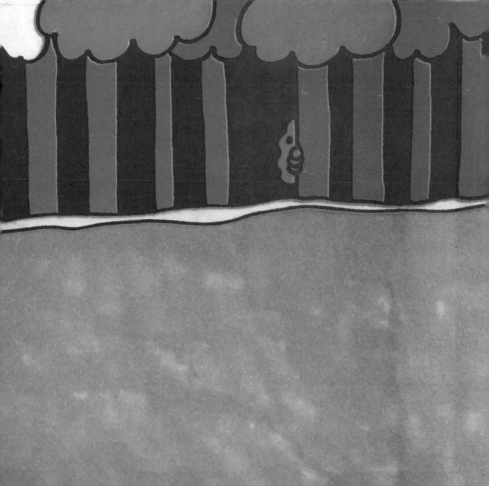

In the long grass in the middle of the field, unseen by Mr Jelly, there was a tramp enjoying a sleep in the autumn sunshine.

Mr Jelly picked his way cautiously through the grass.

The tramp, fast asleep, snored.

"What was that?" shrieked Mr Jelly. "It's a lion!
I heard it growl! Oh goodness gracious! Oh dear
me! A lion! A huge lion! A huge lion with enormous
teeth! A huge lion with sharp teeth that's going to
bite me in two! A huge ferocious lion with
enormous sharp teeth that's going to bite me in two,
if not three!"

And he fainted.

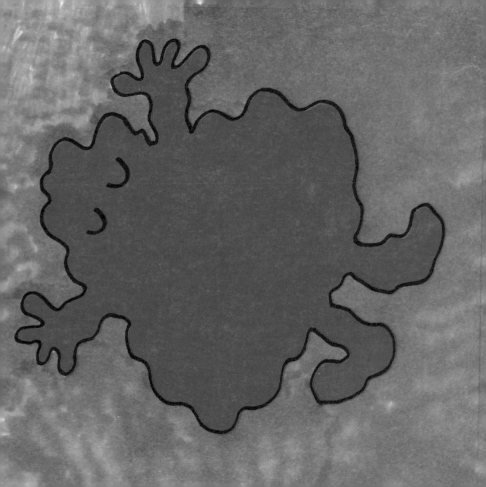

All this commotion awakened the tramp, who yawned, stretched, sat up and saw Mr Jelly lying on the ground beside him.

"Oh dear," he said, for he was a kindly tramp. "Oh dear." And he picked up Mr Jelly and placed him gently in the palm of his hand.

Mr Jelly came to, and sat up rubbing his eyes.

Then he saw the tramp's face looking at him.

"Oh disaster!" he screamed. "Oh calamity! It's a giant! An ogre! Oh gracious! He's going to have me for breakfast!"

"My, my," said the tramp gently. "You're a nervous little chap, aren't you? What's your name?"

"Mr J . . . J . . . J . . . J . . . J . . . J . . . Jelly," stammered Mr Jelly.

"I used to be nervous like you," said the tramp, "but I learned how not to be! Would you like me to tell you the secret?"

Mr Jelly quivered and shook and said, "YYY . Y . . . Yes. P . . . P . . . P . . . Please."

"It's very simple," continued the tramp. "All you have to do is count up to ten, and you'll find that whatever's frightening you isn't quite so frightening after all!"

Then he set Mr Jelly gently down on the grass.

"Remember," he said to Mr Jelly. "Count to ten!" And off he went.

Mr Jelly thought that it would be a very good idea if he went home immediately.

Back across the field he went.

Back through the woods he went.

He was walking through the woods when he stepped on a little twig.

Snap! went the twig.

Mr Jelly jumped twice his own height in terror.

"What was that?" he shrieked. "That terrible snapping noise? It's a tree falling down that's going to crush me to pieces! Oh calamity! It's a crocodile hiding in the bushes snapping its teeth! Oh disaster! It's . . ." And then he stopped.

He took a deep breath.

"Onetwothreefourfivesixseveneightnineten!" he said.

And saw that what had gone snap was a twig. A silly old twig.

"Phew!" he said.

Mr Jelly had almost reached his house when a leaf drifted gently down from a tree, on top of him.

"Help! Police! Murder!" he screamed. "I'm being kidnapped! Oh calamity! It's ruffians! With guns! They're going to . . ." And then he stopped.

He took a deep breath.

"Onetwothreefourfivesixseveneightnineten!"

And then he saw what had fallen on him was only a leaf.

Nothing but a leaf!

A stupid red leaf!

"It works," he said out loud in wonderment.

And do you know, it did work.

After that moment, Mr Jelly became a changed man.

Well, you can see that by looking at him, can't you?

And he never shrieks, or shouts, or screams, or quivers, or shakes, or trembles any more.

And he never hides under the bedclothes any more.

Well.

Not very often, anyway!